MW01520902

# Beautiful

# Tragedies

## Vol II

*A Dark Poetry Anthology*

*Compiled and Edited by*

# XTINA MARIE

HellBound Books Publishing LLC

## +Acknowledgements

Thank you to all of the wonderful poets who contributed to this beautiful anthology. I dare say that this volume is even better than the last, and I am so very excited to be able to share these beautifully tragic words with the world.

Thank you to James Longmore, who gave me full reign with this project.

A special thank you to Denise Jury, who always catches typos that I can't see.

And last but not least, thank you to all of the people and instances in our lives that have *done us wrong* and therefore inspired these tragically beautiful words of ours.

-X

HellBound Books Publishing LLC

# Table of Contents

*Veronica Kegel-Giglio*
And He Killed Me
My Lovely Deadly Love
She Was My Love

*K.H.*
Lithium
Game of Love
Never Have I Ever
Gaslighter
Daddy's Crazy Little Monster

*Maggie D. Brace*
Exquisite Beauty

*A.J. Chilson*
Darkness

*Alex De-Gruchy*
Straight and True

*Lydia Chatelain & Glen Damien Campbell*
Forgive Me, Father

*P.J. Reed*
Separations
A senryu series explaining the most common causes of separations

*John Grey*
Having Fallen in Love with the Children's Nanny

Below her – an aural beyond (hard cut)

*Jamie Zaccaria*
Rumpelstiltskin
Red
Prince Charming

*Marissa Garofalo*
Pain
Caged
Glass Soul

*Clare Castleberry*
Fulfilled
Stalker
Cracked

*John Kojak*
My Heart
Sour Milk
Shit Happens

*Denise Jury*
No More
Unseen
Seeds
Heal
Knife
Once

*Melysza Jackson*

HellBound Books Publishing LLC

Better
Gold
Still
Power

*J.B. Toner*
Winter Rain
Goin' to the Chapel

*Theresa Scott-Matthews*
The Dark Rose

*James Eric Watkins*
These Hands

*Dinner Bell*
Lloyd Lee Barnett

*Aurora Starr*
Walk Amongst the Tombstones
The Mask
Revenge is Sweet
Charade
Someone I Used to Know
My Beating Heart

*James G. Carlson*
The Thing in the Walls
Sever

*Sara Tantlinger*

She Walks in Blood

*Xtina Marie*
…and the Fear
Fingerpainting
My Incubus
Rubbernecking
Right or Wrong
Run
Mother Nature
Your Demonic Creep

HellBound Books Publishing LLC

*How beautiful the tragic seems ...*
                  - Lydia Zinovieva-Annibal

HellBound Books Publishing LLC

# Black Widow

*Alistair Cross*

Her hand stretches out to me
With grace but without motion
As I stumble into nothingness
She offers me her potion
~
I could not see her face
But I knew I knew her well
"Drink from me," she whispered
"I promise not to tell…"
~
Casting a shadow of liquid light
That filtered through the day
I inherit her philosophies
And silently obey
~
While I recited childhood lullabies
Low and languidly
I tasted her thick poison
But first it tasted me
~
In a deadly poetic coma
Into numbness I was anchored
And with barely the strength to whisper
I smiled and I thanked her

HellBound Books Publishing LLC

# The Demon Barber of Fleet Street

*Alistair Cross*

Cloaked figures fill the storm-darkened walks
And shapelessly pass by the parade of signs and shops

When by the light of lamp... from the corner of my
eye
Something in the barber's shop did I peripherally espy:

A flash of something silver; a splash of cherry red
And 'I think I need a shave' thought I... the day I lost
my head

# Final Digital Zoom Meeting

*Robert Fleming*

i was fine, offline, i was
chatting my cat out of its hat
entered zoom, on a web surfers' broom
muted my voice, muted my video
hands raised greet, meet other participants
greetings in the meeting to Satan, jason, freddy,
pazuzu, snake
Satan & pazuzu mute video to show a red slash
jason & freddy click 3 red dots, to show their
name as blank
snake unvideowed to video to a gray square
i am displayed, afraid, in the center zoom box
bordered with blank boxes showing red slashes
i am lost in zoom, my doom awaits
oh moderator, por favor, be my savior

Satanist, sam, I am, surfaces:
u r not on the invitee list 4 Satan's zoom meeting
once u enter, u can exit with a Satan exit pass
get u an exit pass?
sam, i am, am uncertain
Satan's so sick
sin so Satan shall survive

in hell its covid-19 2
its souls 6' separated, & zoom meetings 2
sam, sad i am, no green eggs in hell
stay 4 the meeting?  could be healing?
agenda is hell zoom changes:
change share screen to scare screen
what is your zoom?
zoom in or zoom out?

# Elevator of Blood

## *Robert Fleming*

Such a set setup:
        make 1000 gallons of blood,
                red dye, red dye, red dye!
contain blood, in buckets;
Kubrick commands:
        *Make enough blood 4 10 takes!*
        *Don't let the blood drip into the gap!*
*ACTION!*
Drain the blood on the elevator floor.
*CUT!*
Supermop the floor, for the next take,
*Cut! MORE blood! Action!*
*Cut! LESS blood! Action!*
*Stanley smiles, Tomkins, the Blood's, right;*
*FINAL CLOT!*
UCLA film school did not teach me,
        how to remove a blood wave,
                from delivered egg carpet!
Next setup:
        the twins tricycling,
                on the yellow carpet,
                        and linoleum floor:
*Extract the blood drops from the carpet!*
*SHINE the linoleum!*
*Stanley says, Jack, start Shining!*

*Tomkins says, Tricycle Set's Set*
*Kubrick screams:*
> *Twins on Tricycles, Take #1,*
> *Alcott shoot,*

*ACTION!*

# blood sets the record straight

*Robert Fleming*

human, i am in your veins,
i claimed the nile,
all your statin claims unclot my clots –
i am body sap,
commanded by ur blasted heart –
por favor, stop beating,
let me b still,
stop pushing me around –
whatever, you call my elements,
corpuscles, hemoglobin,
enough, let me b,
por favor, don't stop me
from leaving your vessel, no bandaids
& don't drain me on dirt

# Hurter Wannabee

*Robert Fleming*

applied 2 b a healer
all the angels wanted me
bored with goodness
refused

applied 2 b a hurter
bent on badness
all the hurters refused me
had 2 train

prove 2 the hurters
how I widle a stick in 2 a ruler
how I land the ruler on knuckles
how I make a pain stick
how I push a pain stick sore
how I joined the Grim Reapers, in training

re-applied 2 be a hurter
hurters hurt me
on parting, prince pain giver advised:
   hurt yourself 1st

# lyryP

## *Robert Fleming*

ur in the fangs of the crocodile
you've the crocodile in your fangs

ur body draining out blood
you've blood draining into your body

ur living, but want death
your death, but want living

ur being released
your released from being

ur life is over
ur over life

# Mears

*Robert Fleming*

swiss cheezze holes
sylvester's whiskers
cartoon transformed
low wall hole
orkan denim 1-piece jumpsuit
barn corners
caged wheel
peanut butter metal seesaw
human screams
house hole flash light

# Smoke and Mirrors Wonderland

*Brian James Lewis*

Some days just suck
and that's okay
I just need to make it
through this day
and I'll be all right
Until I think of you

Many nights I drink
myself to sleep
which only proves
that I'm in too deep
and there's no way
to turn this mess around

I drive mile after mile
seeing your face and weep
about what might have been
Smoking the cigarettes that I keep
hidden in the glovebox
one after another, rolling on

My mom worries a lot
and tells me I should
have quit smoking years ago

when I lied that I would
But I'm damn glad
I never did

Otherwise I'd be
doing something worse
and get zero breaks at work
I always take my purse
so I can hit the liquor store
for shots I slam in the bathroom

Many nights I
rave senselessly
in front of my TV
wishing for God to let me
step through the glass and
into that mirrored world inside

Where no one dies
and families stay together
smiling and happy in
marriages that last forever
Unlike miserable reality
that kicks me in the teeth daily

The siren song of escape
keeps getting clearer
beckoning me closer
There's nothing to fear
Just a sweet release
and oblivion deep inside

But my daughter
She needs me more
than ever these days
Walking out the door
just might raze what's left
of our family bonds

Another drink will
make hard reality bend
The television greets me
like an old friend
I'm so fucking lonely
and need to get inside

Someone is screaming
and it hurts my ears
I get a good running start
as my savior appears
Then my face crashes
right through the glass

Wonderland come to me!
Block out the world-Set me free!
This is certainly our finest hour
My legs are dancing mindlessly
Turn on the kaleidoscope machine
Never again will I be alone

# Heat Lightning

*Brian James Lewis*

I sit here on this cold night
Alone, but missing you
and all the things we used to do
The laughter we shared
Kept the bad world at bay
As we hid out in your hideaway
Nothing fancy or flashy
Just a bedroom with a TV
and a mattress just right for you and me
Holding you while you slept
like a baby in my arms, snoring
Your head on my shoulder in the morning
The sun rising as we went down
Into a dream land with hidden nightmares
That sprung upon us as we lay unaware
Because things weren't exactly ideal
Even though we sure wished for them to be
Reality reared its ugly head and made it hard for
me
Not to ask questions or be afraid
When you loved me, but pushed me away
Preferring to keep me at a distance and not say
The words I needed to hear
From the lips in your beautiful face
Painted with makeup to hide every trace
Of sadness, fear, abuse, and addiction

Mental illness, chronic pain, mood swings
A boat broken loose from its moorings
That we are both stuck in
But my kindness and compassion were denied
Your makeup fixed nothing, but damn it, I tried
Our love was fast and strong
Like heat lightning on a mid-July night
Something not made to last, though it felt right
Now I sit alone on this cold night
Freezing to death and wishing in vain
That a rewind button existed to fix our pain

# Just Like Glass Breaks

*Brian James Lewis*

Just like glass breaks
when thrown by angry fingers
Without enough alcohol to
make them happy
My heart lies in smithereens
On the dirty ground, glistening
I want to smile
and say it's okay, but I can't
Hell, I don't even have a clue
Anything good has slipped away
Run out of that broken thing
Just like blood out of the other
Want some advice
That you didn't ask for?
Well here it is my friends
Never be a "nice guy or gal"
Those people just end up alone
detritus left over from a car crash
We are taught by
Good parents, uncles, aunts
How to treat others and love
without expecting much in return
It's such a beautiful fallacy
That works for a select few
I know that some
may have reason to disagree

But on the long-term plan
That's how things go for me
Believe my words when I say
That I hope your life refutes me
Just like glass breaks
My heart lies in smithereens
On the dirty ground, glistening
and there's not enough alcohol
To ever make me smile again
When love's gone, nobody's happy

# No Magic Here

*Brian James Lewis*

I didn't make any promises
When you invited me into your bed
And you were nowhere near honest with me
Things went from lonely hearts having fun
To "let's make a baby" too damn quick
For any of this to be about love
I'm just the guy who's here to hurt the last guy
Who was here to hurt the guy before him
In this crazy, bullshit world you made up
About yourself being some kind of victim
Of "bad guys" who were always untrue
But, I'm not another burned out stoner
Or drug addled, alcoholic, weed head
Who doesn't know what to do
And I'm sure as hell not going to be
Just another one of the guys
Who committed suicide over you
There's no magic here
Just sadness and pain
Built up by years of madness
From telling the same lies again and again
Crying crocodile tears that grow insecurities in men
Well fuck that noise, you're not Barbie and I ain't Ken
Rolling on down the road-For me, it's time
To leave this blazing train wreck far behind
You wanted to own me, but I woke up in time
To see that your sugar is covered in ashes and grime
Not to mention all the flies that live in your bedroom

Paradise was lost, not found
When you thought you had me bound
Hook line and sinker to the bottom of the pond
Making drug buys with my car
It was clear we weren't getting very far
Without your harem of men tagging along

# Estate Sale

*N.M. Brown*

Have you heard the story of Adia Brown?
Her legend haunts the entire town.

She went mad with depression and lack of desire.
Adia doused her home in gas, and set it on fire.

And if that may not sound sinister to you,
What if I told you there were sleeping children
inside too?

Three little darlings; a girl and two boys
Their small faces melted, like the plastic on their
toys.

Fire department was called, they took time to
arrive.
The chances were null that they'd find them alive.

People said the smoke killed them first, but who
can be sure.
 They could have been conscious; searing agony
most pure.

Adia took her life with a gun before the cops
came.

The final straw of sanity snapped, from the
weight of the shame.

A few rooms survived, the children's mainly
being affected.
The debris was cleaned up; the home's items
collected.

An estate sale was held at the end of July.
Towns folk would drop in and find new things to
buy.

My uncle bought a toaster, not knowing it was
cursed.
The first time he used it, he ended up in a hearse.

The buyers of clothes all succumbed to choking.
Adia's canoe on the wall, new owners bodies'
permanently soaking.

Kitchen utensils missed their targets, ever vigilant
and ready.
Appliances bought never plugged in securely or
steady.

As for me, I was given a baby monitor from there.
The sentiment of the gesture was meant with great
care.

Sinister voices appear out of nowhere at night.
They chant at my baby until I turn on the light.

My mind wakes with scorched senses, it smells like something is burning.
 The thick smell of smoke sets my stomach to churning.

Running to my baby's room, I gasp out in surprise.
A normal room greets me, no flames lick at my eyes.

The house never feels hot, just smoky and thick.
My subconscious paranoia; towards me is trying to trick.

If you bought something from Adia, please run now while you can.
Because today… flames very real, are licking at my hand.

# Drink Your Coffee

*N.M. Brown*

The mornings are long and the nights are short
My good intentions are met with a hateful snort
*I've made some coffee Dear*

The children are wild yet you stay asleep
I'm locked away, your prize to keep
*I've made some coffee Dear*

My family calls, you snatch away the phone
You keep me isolated, make sure I'm yours alone
*I've made some coffee Dear*

My spirit more alive than you allow
I have to get us out somehow
*I've made some coffee Dear*

Foundation covers the bruises you've brought
Road maps of scars from where we've fought
*I've made some coffee Dear*

The blood on my lip, a brownish red
You leave for someone's else's bed
*I've made some coffee Dear*

You've ruined our daughter's opinion of men
Up she will grow, not to trust again

*I've made some coffee Dear*

You make the money so you say you'd get the
kids
Visions of your abuse dance behind our eyelids
*I've made some coffee Dear*

You allow me no friends, no family to talk to
My darling sweetheart if you only knew
*I've made some coffee Dear*

I want to fly but you've cut my wings
You indulge in all of your silly flings
*I've made some coffee Dear*

I stand to leave; beaten, battered and low
Your hand a vice on my neck as I try to go
*I've made some coffee Dear*

You scream at the children, I hold them close
I protect them from your hateful blows
*I've made some coffee Dear*

Our eyes not allowed to cry
Your mouth, always telling a lie
*I've made some coffee Dear*

All of us under your control
Oppression being your main goal
*I've made some coffee Dear*

You tear us down and keep us there
No other marriage that can compare
*I've made some coffee Dear*

I thought you'd want the best for us
You only wanted the best OF us
*I've made some coffee Dear*

There is no love in the way that we mate
You thrust into me, I feel the hate
*I've made some coffee Dear*

Every morning I paste on a smile
I try my best to love you all the while
*I've made some coffee Dear*

Your cold breakfast sits on the table
Our new life starts as soon as we're able
*I've made some coffee Dear*

Ground up ricin; a tasteless bean
You like your coffee, strong black and mean
*I've made your coffee Dear*

It's hard to acquire but easy to use
I will free myself from these years of abuse
*I've made some coffee dear*

A helpless victim used to be where I once stood
A warrior now, in our house in the wood
*I've made some coffee Dear*

We will step over you on our way out the door
I won't let them see their Daddy laying on the
floor
*I've made you coffee Dear*

I'm smarter than you think I am
Never again a door will you slam

***Drink your coffee Dear***

# Wolf

## *N.M. Brown*

The wolf is going to eat me, I see him start to roam
The wolf is going to eat me, I'm long far away from home

The wolf is going to eat me, its breath fogs heavy in the night
The wolf is going to eat me, I've no chance to survive a fight

The wolf is going to eat me, in the woods on Valentine's Day
The wolf is going to eat me, I have no meat to keep it away

The wolf is going to eat me, its caught my scent and slowed
The wolf is going to eat me, to our date my husband never showed

The wolf is going to eat me, the moon is full and bright
The wolf is going to eat me, its teeth glisten in the moonlight

The wolf is going to eat me, I'm far too slow to run
The wolf is going to eat me, it hunts me just for fun

The wolf is going to eat me, my flesh it will tear apart

The wolf is going to eat me, meat sweetened by the
fear in my heart

The wolf is going to eat me, it is inches from me now
The wolf is going to eat me, it licks the sweat from off
my brow

The wolf is going to eat me, with breath hot, muggy
and thick
The wolf is going to eat me, it pins my foot as I try to
kick

The wolf is going to eat me, that is no surprise
The wolf is going to eat me, and he has my husband's
eyes

# Never Wanted

## *Brianna Malotke*

The grandfather clock in the hall goes off
Every hour, on the hour, and every sound it makes
Echoes throughout the house – echoes in my heart –
For though this grand Victorian is full of beautiful
and ornate furniture, baroque art, and anything
You could ever want in the world,
You've never wanted me.

And so, I sit, all alone,
Night after night,
Listening to the old clock strike,
Tallying my hours spent here, collecting dust
Amongst the items you've chosen,
Though you've never once chosen me.

My heart aches, sorrow has taken permanent residence
In my bones, my movements ghost like,
Drifting from room to room, moving silently
As I wander through your vast assortment
Of items you've hand-picked over the years,
Yet you've never once picked me.

One day I will wilt and fade away,
Cast aside like any other broken thing,
My heart withered over time, will cease to beat,
And so, though you've never desired me,
I will be a permanent piece of your collection,
My spot in your mind everlasting, for one day

You will miss my faithful companionship.

# Painted Lady

*Brianna Malotke*

Our forever home, a now faded
painted lady, once vibrant,
now a little worn around the edges,
was nestled on a spacious lot,
tucked in among the evergreens.

The paint was chipped,
Landscaping too overgrown,
Just everything about this once
Austere and grand Victorian
Home was now faded.

Its glory days long gone.
No one would come for tea
And gossip in the sitting room.
No more lavish dinner parties
With records playing until dawn.

Sun damaged colors, and tired
Looking décor, this striking home
Now sits deserted, for when you left
You took the heart with you,
And I too will fade with it, until
Nothing is left but bare bones.

# The Fate of Heartache

*Brianna Malotke*

Taking a long drag, her mind wandered,
The end of her cigarette illuminated
The once joyful room around her,
As she sat silently in the darkness.

The windows were open, and somewhere
Off in the distance, there were crickets
Chirping periodically, but the silence
Lingered here in this empty room.

She took a slow inhale – and exhale – as smoke
Hovered around her face, thoughts of them
Together swirled in her mind, and dissipated
With the smoke, the loneliness overwhelming.

Soft shadows danced along the walls, the dim
glow
Of her last cigarette fading, ending any minute,
Feeling the crisp autumn air, chilly against
Her bare skin, as she sat alone in the darkness.

He was never coming back, and no matter
What she tried – séances or Ouija boards
or spirits – no one could offer guidance,
He was gone from her forever.

Their two souls now drifting, lost
From the other's for eternity, she sighed
And rubbed out her cigarette, finished
With it and everything holding her here.

A grim decision was made that evening,
With the extinguishment of the cigarette,
Everything clicked into place, and she knew
How they could be together evermore.

As the ashes smoldered and died, she took hold
Of her fate – cutting her string much earlier
than the three fates had planned – and welcomed
Her love with open arms in the afterlife.

# And He Killed Me

*Veronica Kegel-Giglio*

I had such a hard time getting over the demise of my last love

I felt lonely and depressed and decided to join a dating service to move on with life I gave all my energy to creating the best want ad possible

And then he answered my ad and met me at the local tavern

He said he was smitten with me from the start and would not stop calling me He even followed me to work, school, shopping, and the movies

Others told me to beware because obsessive love could be dangerous.

When he was angry with me, he became a vile ugly monster, and he could be evil

He did not like me calling friends especially men friends His face changed shape and his skin changed color when he got angry

Veins popped out of his neck, and his eyes bulged

When he was not angry, he was sweet and bought me gifts

Others told me to be careful

I found out he had been with other girls who had-disappeared

I should have known better when he told me I had to come with him to see his secret place

I should have sensed what he would do

However, I wanted him to keep taking care of me

So I followed him into those woods

And that's where he told me I was never allowed to leave him

There he killed me by hacking me up into a hundred pieces

And now I haunt these woods trying to warn others

I warn them not to try to love him

# My Lovely Deadly Love
*Veronica Kegel-Giglio*

I was man enough to admit she always made me
hot

She drove me crazy with her feminine wiles

I took her to the most expensive restaurants and
bought her jewels

She could never get enough sex, and I loved that
about her

I never had felt so much for any female I met
online

However, she had lots of secrets and talked in
riddles

She then took me to her home in an abandoned
theater basement

There she turned into a vile monster with horrible
eyes and foul breath

I saw she ate babies and cast spells on others
while worshipping Satan

She told me not to fear her and that I must love
her forever

She wanted me to become like her

However, I could not let that happen

She was a thing of the undead

I could not let her turn me into something
unhuman

So I killed myself instead

I could not let her change me

# She Was My Love

*Veronica Kegel-Giglio*

She was the great love of my life

However, she insisted that I could only see her at night

Her name was Delilah and the sex with her was like no other

We met in the parking lot by her work

She was sweet to me but ended up biting and beating me

Delilah's eyes, teeth, smell, and moans were sweet

However, she made me lie and steal for her once we had sex

After meeting her my life was hexed.

She told me I was the best girlfriend she'd ever had

And she had had both male and female lovers

However, I could not pull away from her and I could not forget her

I wanted to be only with her, but I could never satisfy her

She wanted more and more from me

That was just too much you see

She haunted and stalked me

Because she could not let me go even though I did not make her happy enough

She taunted and mocked me

So I had to kill her you see

I cut off her head and I buried it you see

Because such a creature can never love or give

Such a being only takes and takes

I could not let her suck away my life

# Lithium

*K.H.*

I'm not living…
There's moving air in my lungs
But I'm not breathing
There's a heart pounding in my chest
But it's not beating
There isn't a pulse
There's no electricity in my skull
My brain is numb
I'm just a walking corpse
A walking zombie
These pills they gave me
They fed me
Promise to God they told me
Would make it all better
But the bees are buzzing
My head is numbing
My brain is busting
My lungs are rushing
My veins are bursting
My life… hush
Lithium

# Game of Love

## K.H.

No one has ever loved me
Until it was too late
They never took my hand
And danced with me in the rain
My heart was at war
And my soul was the battlefield
I wanted more
I wanted them to feel
And when they realized
That my heart was all they wanted
My soul had moved on
To closets that were less haunted
And every time I walk out,
I get reeled straight back in
Because nothing hurts better
Than this love sick game of sin
Where another led me by the heart
While they took me by the hand
This cyclic game of love
That started from wedding bands

# Never Have I Ever
*K.H*

"Never have I ever… broken my heart."
Looks at him
"This is where you raise your glass
and drink."

# Gaslighter
*K.H.*

Today I stopped loving you
After all the shit you've put me through
I packed a bag and whispered a goodbye
Finally tired of all your lies
I'm tired of all your fucking abuse
Just because you don't hit me
Doesn't mean your words don't bruise
It's always about your needs
Never fucking mind about mine
It's all a twisted game to you
A quick sick fuck of the mind
And I'm getting tired of your gaslighting
And your shit don't stink attitude
Mama's little fucking boy
Expecting the world to bend over
Taking it from you
And even after the venting
And crying on the bedroom floor
I still don't have the fucking strength
To walk out that god damned door

# Daddy's Little Crazy Monster

*K.H.*

I have scars even though you may not see them
There has been a razor ran down my arm
You just can't see it
Every time I have been blamed
Yelled at, lied to, spat at, cursed
Degraded
Called a whore
Called a worthless bitch
Every time I don't think I deserve to be here
You couldn't count the times I have wished
That I could just end it all
Everything just floats down the drain
All the pain, disdain
Everyone don't wear their scars on their skin
Some people tote their scars deep within
Some people bury the words others have thrown
And build a glass house made from their sticks
and stones
But me I just draw an imaginary line
Wipe the blood from my lip and smile
Daddy's little crazy monster pops another pill
And floats down the path wondering what is real.

# Exquisite Beauty
*Maggie D. Brace*

My body lies enrapt by your exquisite beauty,
yet my soul recoils in horror.
As our evenings spent rolling in ecstasy end,
my heartache just becomes sorer.

Each day I promise to stand resolute and firm
to end our association.
Yet each night brings a new height of joy,
that renews my fascination.

They say our love can only harm us,
and others along the way.
It doesn't matter who we take down,
it's a price I'm willing to pay.

The dichotomy of our surreal romance
has torn me asunder.
But I'm willing to accept our love/hate,
I'll stick with my true blunder.

# Darkness

*A.J. Chilson*

Darkness is looming,
Satan is grooming.

The visions are real,
Painfully surreal.

Is this where I go?
Nice glories I throw.

All for brief pleasure
Over great treasure.

I wish I had thought
On what I must not.

Was it all worth it?
The pain I now get.

No second chances,
Just consequences.

# Straight and True

*Alex De-Gruchy*

Go and shoot me down, my darling, go on and
shoot me down
If you're walking out that door, if you're not
hanging around
You better pull that trigger if you mean what you
say
Because without you here by my side then I'm
done today

The void inside that barrel doesn't scare me at all
This sickening terror comes from the thought I let
you fall
Right through my fingers, and all the while I
couldn't tell
If it's true then cutting me down is far kinder than
this hell

I held you through the good times and I held you
through the bad
Thought I was wise but I never knew someone
could feel this sad
So much for "I'll love you forever", like
everything else it dies
And right now I'd choose death over the tears in
your eyes

If my sunshine's setting and all I've got left is this
hurt
If the things I believed were really just delusions
and dirt
If in the end none of it means a single fucking
thing
I'll still be hearing your sweet voice as you make
that gun sing

Do one last thing for me, my love, and aim
straight and true
For this breaking heart that for so long beat just
for you
Once it was just bruised but now you're tearing it
in two
So let it fall silent as I fall, if we're really through

# Forgive Me, Father

*Lydia Chatelain & Glen Damien Campbell*

Forgive me, Father, for I have sinned
I have sinned for I have loved
With all my heart
With all my soul
With all my body
I have adored and worshipped

I have given my heart – and it was squandered
I have given my soul – and it was misplaced
I have given my body – and it was ill-treated

All that's left is painful memories
My love was innocent
Pure and true

Forgive me, Father, for I once believed
That you loved me as I loved you
That the world was full of devotion and happiness
That humanity was not faithless and profane!

# Separations

A senryu series explaining the most common
causes of separations
*P.J. Reed*

busy businessman
writes his wife a postcard while
sexting a friend

rotund man wobbles
after disappointed wife
carrying a spoon

he dreams of monsters
stories float on empty pages
still his wife talks on

hungry young father
hunts melted cheese toastie prey
wife stands forgotten

tired businessman
takes ageing wife to dinner
hungry for a change

on husband watching
jealous wife sweeps to his side
brushes girls away

# Having Fallen in Love with the Children's Nanny

*John Grey*

Let the water take hold of the body,
pull that corpse down to its depths,
a mere outline written on its surface,
before it ripples away to all shores.

Please, let her remain at lake bottom,
no phony reanimation,
no rancid color in those pale cheeks,
no sudden lightness, no cheating gravity.

I don't want her floating on the surface,
drifting where the wind makes current,
until her limp, bloated purple-skinned body,
thumps against the dock, the rowboat.

I fear those cold eyes fixed in permanent stare,
breeze nestling in her nostrils like breath,
a lizard crawling from her mouth as if she's
speaking,
a hand bobbing on the surface like it's reaching
out to me.

I know she's dead.
But what if she doesn't look the part?

# The Making of a Vampire: The Cemetery

*Jen Ricci*

The rain fell
On the very border of madness
Caged somewhat, somewhat in myself
It was a terrifying prospect
To face death in such a successful manner
Of sort – so
Madness of thought
The million voices of the dead
Silent
Audible where my steps
Met the wet grass
Utter madness to think, only think
To raise above one's station
Turning the probable end
Into this unwanted eternity
Of thought and utter thirst of blood.
Be MY sacrifice
Like in a trance he looked at me, obedient
And I smiled
Knowing all to well that there was no joy
He could not care
He was not THERE.
On the border of rationality and the empty shell
That was his ROBOTIC body

He lay on a Victorian epitaph
Oh the irony! It said, "Beloved wife!"
So I shall be, the fangs cutting his neck deep
While the red beauty of gore
Free flowing warm kiss of death
And eternal life
Repulsive gift bestowed on the unlucky
Forever dead.

# Darkness is My Eternal Mother

*Jen Ricci*

Inner darkness
Why so dark
Why You, Mother?
I want to see in you all
That IS
Wholesome and good
And you are a
MONSTER
I'll escape and suffer this truth
The son of the vampire,
Is that what you are, mother?
Here's a concept for you
The inevitability of CORRUPTION
Of becoming the very vampire YOU are
Groomed since birth in knowing the opulent evil
Of repeated trauma
Foreign lands known all to well
The overbearing duplicity of HYPOCRISY
Inner darkness in the DNA of our lives
Mothers should love
Not devour.

# The Vampire
## *Michael Perret*

## I

### Dreams of Decadence

It's not so much a coffin, where I sleep
But a bath where I do not doze, I steep
Thinking and scheming and plotting a drink
Submerging and letting all my thoughts sink
         into a pool of blood…

         …and, in my dreams, the flood
Fills my mouth and my throat, and warms my skin
Like wine, once upon a time, from within
Until half-mad and excited with thirst
I stir, cadaverous, starved and accursed –

## II

### Tears of Wine

The blood in my glass looks like chocolate wine.
The film inside creeps down like long fingers...
Shadows on the wall, the shame that lingers
From the night before, both foul and fine

In the moonlight – They want it, and I laugh.
Children – no – pets, cattle, blood bags that calve
More wineskins, you want what you cannot have...
The check for this drink is your epitaph!

Still, they stare, they watch it swell at my lips!
I am beautiful, and desire craves
The forbidden not in sips, but in waves
Till it burns like poison, courses and rips –

Come... Don't just taste the unknown with your eyes –
Have a sip, but not from my glass, try this...
And when you wake up, remember whose kiss
Made you an undead distiller of cries.

## III

### Self-Portrait in a Still Life

I am a plucked rose in a vase of blood,
A still life in a frame and beyond time,
A dead piece of nature in meter and rhyme
I soak up eternity in a flood

Of dead men and women, the vital mud
This flower needs to enrich its sublime
And singular beauty; forever, I'm
One futureless bloom, not a single bud –

And if on occasion I nick the vein
That surges down a ridged cock when its thick,
Or pierce with my fangs lips I tease and lick,

It's not for the sex, but for the warm spurt
In my mouth – of ecstasy – as I drain
Their bodies and leave them dry and inert.

## IV

## Danse Macabre – Desiccated Extremity

You'll want to see it, but will fade to black
       Before your desire can have its way –
At the touch, through my clothes, you'll start, pull back
       But swept up in my swift waltz of dismay

You'll succumb, unsatisfied and the lack
       Will haunt your visions slowly sucked away
Where confused, maybe you'll blame the cognac,
       Then writhe in my arms, then lilt and then sway –

       The thing you died wanting was old and dried,
Desiccated into a hairy root –
It putrified first, like a rotting fruit;

       But vampires, when they die as women, hide
Wilted black petals that keep their perfume
And impregnate their tomb's still, stale vacuum –

# V

## Sonnet à l'anglaise

I have no regrets, my immortal ways
Suit me and I miss nothing of the past
My future's an eternal present, stays
Like a dream, untimed, my days and nights last

Forever, untouched by the hours' haste
Slow, they are decadent, I take my time
Pleasure when squandered is the only waste
I know, to me mortality's a crime.

But that doesn't mean I don't sometimes feel,
Out of boredom if not some other need,
A longing for something new and unreal
Calling me forth to create, intercede

And, proud of the things I have and will sire,
Abort nature with a newborn vampire.

# Burst

*K. Demmans*

A heart so hollow
Burst forcibly inside you
It echoes with grief

# If I Become Her

*K. Demmans*

You say you won't tell me
'Cause then I might leave you
I know that you hurt her
And it consumes you
You see her heart break
Each time your eyes close
She's in too many pieces
For you to pick up
A story so burning
It threatens your past
Your trail still blazing
As you still move on
You say that you love me
But now I'm just waiting
Until I become her

# Repeat to Myself

*K. Demmans*

I never loved you
I never cared
I never liked your hands through my hair
You said my name so sweet
But the way you hurt me felt so deep
And how you let me down
I thought that I would drown
The pain you caused me stung so much
That my heart just blew up
So to piece me back together
I have to tell myself that
I never loved you
I never cared

# Wedding in the Woods

*Madison Estes*

Her hand protrudes from the soil,
as though begging to be kissed,
while an earthworm wraps around her third digit,
a slimy marriage band.

An array of witnesses come forward, wild deer
and wolves,
that should be our friends and family,
and our forsaken fetus,
but the only life her body can grow now are
maggots and their kind,
the creatures of decomposition.

I regret that this is our wedding in the woods,
our honeymoon of horror,
almost as much as the fact that I put her there.

# Candles

*Madison Estes*

The lightbulb filaments fade out for the final time.
As the burning stick of wax lights my way,
I am reminded of the candles we lit to
unite two separate lives into one.

The candles at this dead-end séance
can't bring you back to me.
If you had only died,
they might stand a chance.

HellBound Books Publishing LLC

# Old Flames Burn Twice

*Madison Estes*

Moth to an old flame
only I am to blame.
I want to move on,
but don't know how.
You were the flame,
and I'm just ashes now.

# Whatever Helps You Sleep At Night
*Madison Estes*

Tell yourself it doesn't matter,
that you didn't know any better,
that no one means the things they say
when they're angry,
that you didn't intend to hurt me,
that it's not (all) your fault,
that you did everything you could
to make things right,
that it's all for the best,
tell yourself whatever it takes
to help you sleep at night

just don't tell yourself the truth.

# All the Lies He Told Me
## *Magnolia Silcox*

I believed all his lies and every single word he said

But it still didn't change the fact that he cheated

It's hard to find out that love is nothing more than a lie

I'd gladly let him burn like a witch at the stake just to see him suffer in pain and slowly die

I'm done hearing his shitty apology

Now I am right next to his bed and he's crying out for me to just leave him be

I gave him my heart so many times just for him to break it again

He better hurry up and finish his last words before I count to ten

He told me that I was special and that I was the only one

If love actually exists then why is there so much pain in my heart that feels like the hot blistering sun

He said that he would marry me in an instant

Now those warm fuzzy feelings I felt are so distant

I'm done with the butterflies swarming around in my stomach

Now the very idea of true love makes me sick

Now the only happiness I feel is when I'm slitting his throat with a knife

Farewell to the man who used to be the so-called love of my life

I think I'll dump his body into a ditch

And he can rot and burn in hell right next to his slutty little bitch

# Friday the Thirteenth

*Gerri R. Gray*

Every day is Friday the thirteenth,
Every night a book of dark curses,
Every heartbeat and every breath,
A countdown to death and its nothingness.
Gray highways paved with the remnants of
dreams,
Shattered, abandoned, forgotten by time,
Twisting and turning like venomed serpents,
Leading to nowhere with signs blurred by pain.
Every kiss is a knife that slices,
Droplets of crimson that spell out your name.
Another sword brandished, another scar:
Each one cuts deeper than the one before.
Every year is a mirror broken,
Every path crossed by black cats of doom,
A lifetime of meanings so meaningless,
Futile and dismal, a gathering storm.

# In the Violet Obscurity

*Gerri R. Gray*

In the violet obscurity of a joyless twilight,
In graveyards I walk alone, echoless,
On carpets of spongy moss and creeping phlox,
Past long-forgotten tombs and nameless crypts
That weep shadows for the death of sunbeams.
A cold wind arises as the orange horizon
Bids a sad farewell.

Memories of you, and of us
Tumble cruelly through my mind
Like windswept leaves, helpless,
Directionless.
Words, like daggers, pierce my heart;
Their poisoned tips swim in my blood,
Tainting the remnants of my hopes.

In the violet obscurity of a joyless twilight,
I hunt with desperation for resolve,
But reflections of things that once were
Are all that I find.
I look to stone sentinels for comfort
But all they can offer is indifference.
And then, bursting up through the dirt,
A clawing hand! Putrid and horrid.
A hand of decomposition.
My hand.

I scream and run,
Trip and fall like the darkness.
My bones shatter. My mind careens.
Silent laughter fills the air
As I feel my insignificance growing
Malignant like a cancer.

I reach out for your hand to help me up
But a frosty wind is all I feel
Biting at my flesh.
I yearn for yesterday
But, like my salvation,
It is buried too deep to exhume.
The sky, now indigo and starry
Becomes a shroud for my corpse.
The netherworld of your eyes
As I remember them
Becomes my open grave.

# My Heart-Shaped Box
## *Gerri R. Gray*

My grief
I conceal in a heart-shaped box
alongside pressed flowers
and broken jewels
and pieces of madness
like satin-wrapped candies,
  too awful to open,
    too savory not to.

Each day
I visit my heart-shaped box
to peer at its treasures
in chambers of blood
so dark and so dreadly
like yesterdays' nightmares,
  too vile to remember,
    too grave for forgetting.

# For a Moment
## *Gerri R. Gray*

I lay on the floor of your empty room
and stared at the ceiling of white,
screaming your name again and again
until my throat burned with fire
and my lips cracked and bled.

You did not answer.

I crawled like a baby,
teary-eyed and broken,
clinging to the past and wishing away today.
For a moment I prayed
for death to take me too.

But all it did was sneer.

One by one, I removed your clothes
from their white plastic hangers
and emptied out your dresser drawers.
Your scent, familiar and sweet,
lingered in the air for a moment.

And then it was gone.

I thought, for a moment, your face I glimpsed
but it was just the shadow of a cloud

moving across the wall.
I thought, for a moment, your voice I heard,
alive and sanguine like before,
but it was just the sage-scented breeze.

And nothing more.

# Taking Care of Business
*Susan Purr*

I breathe, slow-blink. I own this room.
*And Johnny doesn't.*
From spotlights and strobes, blue,
green and gold, to the music,
hot and throbbing.
*He always hated*
"I Put a Spell on You."
*Johnny who?*
I'll sing it loud now.
I own these gawkers stalking
into the bar. They watch me,
long liquid alabaster.
Ring master for these tiger men,
cash-heavy crocodiles, stomping
I'm yours, yours, yours.
*Johnny was a different beast.*
Hands in their pants despite
my fat lip, my purple cheek; I have them
hypnotized. White hands finesse the pole,
*he wanted to kill me,*
my body writhing serpentine.
*struck me from behind,*
I crack the whip,
*finding me here, calling me whore,*
I roll my hips,

*I ran to the bathroom,*
I flip my hair,
           *where he grabbed me*
howling.
           *howling.*
      I smile and snarl and claw the air.
        *He ripped and hit,*
        *ruined lace, my face and spandex.*
Dollars fly, swarming.
        *Sequins scattered on the floor, and the world*
           *gurgled fuzzy gray.*
      *I s*coop money to my breasts,
        *I heard drops of rain,*
        *and felt the change... coming*
and bending low, I show them
        *soaked in sweat, smelling blood.*
what they came to see. Nice and slow,
        *His throat pulsed,*
        *and then was still.*
      Hear the roars! So hungry!
        *My teeth ached. Oh so hungry!*
Liquor flows,
        *I wiped my mouth.*
one more bow, I'll blow a kiss,
        *Johnny who?*
and hurry off to hide the body.

# Let the Bleeding Hearts Fall

*Serena Daniels*

He tore my heart out, it felt so long ago
I've been empty since, numb to everything
Save for feelings of hate and vengeance
Thanks to your teachings, I can sniff out your
kind easily
And I take full advantage of that when I can
Catching them is easy, I just play pretend and wait
I gain satisfaction from the looks on their faces
when I carve out their hearts and drop them
I never look back, only look forward and move
along
I'll keep it up as long as I can and I'll be the better
for it
Because of you I'll be letting the bleeding hearts
fall

# Venus in Retrograde

*Shawn Chang*

In discord shadows foray, flicker, part
Among these catacombic chambers; chains
Ensconce naïve convictions, and my heart—
No longer blind, beguil'd, bemus'd—ordains
Pure vindication. I unsheathe and shed
These knives of knave you'd buri'd in flesh mine;
Reopen scars to here imbibe the lead,
The poisons of consuming odium. Vine
By vine this livid vengeance, groaning, grows,
Alive with smiles. I sever, tress aft tress,
Frail sentiments; elute, discard the prose
You'd made me drink. Emotions evanesce
       In retrograde-Venusian skies; reprieve
       I seek—for you, tonight shall be Death's eve.

# Heaven and Hell

*Gerardo Serrano R.*
To Edith Edyllic or Edith Centipede (whoever she
is or in whatever blessed mood she is)

Now I know,
I haven't realized such a truth
But until this day.
At this moment, in this stingy instant,
That I've got to face it
And give solution to this conundrum,
No matter how impossible it could be.

Everything seems to me
That there are no possibilities for me;
That there never has existed
Or will have existed nothing for me.
Only some instants, seconds,
When I was face to face
With what my soul hankered after so earnestly,
And, for a moment, it seemed to be mine.
But it wasn't true at all.

There were times when I lived like a drudging ant.
Harvesting all I could for the morrow,
The one I was planning eternally,
But this never came to happen
Spoiling all my reserves.

There were other times when I lived
Eating the desert of the present,
But I didn't keep scrums for the future,
And when it came,
I starved.

I ignore the hidden mysteries of science,
The secrets you keep from me.
That was an instant, that was all,
That I waited for and one day came
But soon it left me.
One hoped-for day
One that never arrived.
Now that I think of it: when will it end?
Why will it never end?
Why will it have to be expanded endlessly
That impossible end?
There are voids impossible to fill,
Not even with the texture of ending
That I will never be capable to sense.

I am so different from myself,
I cannot imitate me.
I am faithful to each principle,
I never go further from what I have established.
Waiting has annihilated me,
I'm not the one I used to be,
I have died inside.
Now that I have given my most precious gift,
There is nothing more to believe,
When everything I knew was only a lie.

Why doesn't everybody die
and leave me alone?
Is that too much to ask?
That would be a small favor,
A little bit of compassion for me.

There is no more poetry in me no more,
Not even a word with which
I could make myself be understood.
So I can corroborate
What I am going to say, what I want to say.
I want to die; I want to explode,
Come asunder, as mighty dust.
I want to kill; I want to exterminate;
To spread laments.
I want to enjoy with your dead,
My dearest friend,
The sweetest one, the tenderest one.
I want to find out how your pain is,
I want you to suffer
In the same way that I have.
I want to see you die.

Eviscerate me with your cold crystal sight,
Kill me with the cruelty of a vulture.
End with this insufferable grief,
Turn off the light…
Just kill me,
And die.

Transforming…
Transcending life…
Dying is to give life…
Die, just die
Die for me.

I hate,
You don't know how much I hate you.
I cannot believe in you anymore.
I cannot believe in anybody else.
Die, suffer and endure,
Bleed to death for me.
Leave me alone,
Let me die in this peace,
Let it be undisturbed
Kill me and die,
Go straight to hell.

Taste my hatred,
Savor your greatest masterpiece,
Each sip is bitter as hell.
Don't dare to understand me ever,
Judge me however you please,
Anyway
What I want will never be mine.
I hate so many things
And among them
You are.

# Give Me Just One Reason...

*Gerardo Serrano R.*

Give me just one goddamned reason,
So I keep on being alive;
Yes, tell me, you, who believe to know it all.
Just give me one valid reason, I dare you.
Mysteries you think to know,
And among them
Pick one, the one you think is the best-chosen,
So I could carry on in my cruel destiny
On this wearisome world.

Reasons I need to get,
So this foul reek I can comprehend.
Tell me, why?
If dead I can be more unhassled,
Tell me the portentous truth,
Which can stop me
From pulling the trigger?
Tell me, hoarder of joyful gifts,
The reason why it's lawful to live,
So I don't shot lead against my temple,
And all over the floor, I spread,
All my bloody intelligence.
Tell me why this machine must keep working,
Functioning the scrutinizing eyeballs,

Registering with beams of light
Grotesque human faces.
Tolerating wickedness,
Uncouthness and plain banality,
Which makes me indignant so vilely.

If you truly exist
God,
There, up in heaven, listen to my cry,
I challenge you to strip me from life.
If you're indeed all-merciful
Take this doubt out of me
And take heed of my blasphemy.
Take pity on me, you,
Miserable creature,
And send death toward me,
And order your exterminating angel to finish with
my life.
Why keep on living? What for? Tell it to me.
Alone, why I have to live if I could be dead,
And comfortably in a box dwell,
Getting rotten, quickly, like a corpse,
And not slowly and painfully,
Like I'm rotting now, alive and pathetically.

I want to be transformed into a pile of filthiness.
Tell me why? The death,
The wise equalizer of it all,
Doesn't get even with me, and why not,
To put an end to the whole world and life
For once and for all.

I dream of transforming the mighty human race
Into a stack of putrescence,
And with repulsion the whole universe fill.

There is no more marvelous thing than our human
machinery,
The most perfect
Of all clockworks,
Impossible to be a match is, but, then:
Tell me?
Worshipers of the body,
Why does it have to generate and accrue shit?
 Why does it have to revolt us every day?

Man is the most portentous and abominable thing,
We are nothing but pure vile matter,
Which slowly decays all over the world.
What a beautiful thing it is!
Only a filthy blotch, of all of us,
Will have to remain.

A banquet of maggots is what of all of us will
persist,
Time is a cruel enemy, sooner or later,
Will have to reach us.
Brief, very brief indeed, it'll last the epitome of
our youngness,
Compared, eternal, oldness seems to be
During the dusk of life,
But more insignificant furthermore is,
Compared with death.

# Run All Over Me

*Gerardo Serrano R.*

Run
All over me,
Cos I want to be
Under your feet.

Run
All over me,
Cos under your wheels
I want to be.

If I am nothing, nothing for you,
Does it make any sense to keep living?
Why not, once and for all,
Do you splatter my head and finish with me?
Anomy of life,
Give me my ending,
Don't let me suffer any longer.

Why do you like to make me suffer?
End up with my misery
Once and for all, don't you?
Or don't you think so?
Tell me, don't be quiet,
Don't be like that.

You have to be good,

After all:
Am I not your friend?
But If I am Mr. Nobody,
Why live?

End up once and for all with this trouble,
I only want to die.
To be annulled by you.
If my dreams have lost their owner,
Why, so absurdly, keep going?

I am fragile,
Like a piece of crystal,
With me, you will finish so effortlessly.

So run,
All over me,
Step on at full throttle
Your gas pedal,
And with your almighty car,
Run over me.

Run
All over me,
Cos I want to be
under you.

Run
All over me
Cos under your wheels
I want to die.

I want your headlights
To blind my eyes,
To listen to your humming roaring
Of your hard metal,
In the middle of my sobbings.
To hear your droning engine,
Closer to my face.
To spill all my liquids
All over there.

To feel the impact
Of your grand apparatus,
Spattering all my blood
All over the floor.
I want for a moment,
To burst in ache,
Crushed and to be trampled,
Pouring off my brains on the floor,
I want to stop suffering.

So then… run
All over me,
I want to feel
Your mighty power
All over me.

# Unreal

*Gerardo Serrano R.*

I'm unreal
A reality which lacks matter;
A lie said so subtly
To open a pure heart,
And thus charm it insistently,
Until it deranges its feeble understanding,
And have it helpless and open,
And thus, with precision, tore it apart.

I'm a lost bird
On the Plutonian night.
The terror of those who gravitates
Lost in the murkiness.
An Archangel of acrimony
From whom only wickedness emanates.

I'm cruel and compassionate,
Hard and corrosive;
An spawn of putrefaction
From the glacial nihilist.
I emerged from a mind,
From the primordial confusion.
From an eternal setback
That reigns inside my chest.
A runaway feeling
From the accursed reality

Where I see my weakness.
I am that and also nothingness
--An illusion tangible as smoke
Which emerges from a pyre.

My name is blue
And I'm a fallen angel.
One day I was a 'beautiful light'
But… a wish of being something greater,
Greater than what my powers
Allowed me to materialize,
So much more than what
I could have truly had.
It condemned me to fall into the abyss.
That is why, to hell, I fell over,
To live in its name eternally
And I only allowed to go out
During November nights.

A spawn amused with souls,
Dullard dunces, whose stupidity is abundant;
Taking the most profane to be doomed,
And their misfortune I regret
During the darkness.
My kingdom and world are shadows
Out of them, I'm nothing,
Just another dead soul,
A cadaver that oozes only pity.

I am charlatan and a liar,
Braggart in my own special way;

A weird and sinister being;
I would wolf down the whole of the moon
And the tender fleshes of the sunrise.
There is no sortilege or magic
Able to get rid of me;
Because I will always be here, in your hunger,
Croaking my course to you,
Crying, never, alas, never!
For forever and for the rest of all eternity.

I dream of myself free and unique,
I dream of myself free and untamed,
Ignoring my true nature.

I am the Nocturnal Bird that awakes you at night
During your nightmares;
The one who during your reveries unsettles you.
There are whispers and there are lies,
Blurted out to forget my wretchedness.

My soul lies captive,
From a stiff flesh that represses it,
There are sometimes that I wish I could tear
myself apart
And thus, from rottenness, I would be able to
escape.
Blessed you be, my only escape from necrosis.

# Darkness

*Theresa C. Gaynord*

Pale lips part, titillating the words,
trumped by those assassin eyes that
form the terms of squelched passions,
pursuit facilitated not by a slick,
scrimshaw knife, but by the hands that
once caressed her body with shameful
indulgences.

He cups her neck, tightening the grip,
forgetting how to forgive the abortion
she's just had; pain exorcised the demons
of regret, like a song that weeps for the
past, happy it's remained there. His face is
chiseled ice, the wounds of his soul,
beyond the scope of understanding.

One vacant smile, mute to the invitation
it contains, mute, to his spotlight of misery.
He leaves her once embrace in the raw
mechanics of the act, abstract to the concept
of time. His self-proposal is this: to not waste
any more time, to reestablish the vigor of
his drive within the sanity of proceeding,

to feel, the subliminal and unspoken ease
of pleasant diversion. He writes stories

in a chorus of pleasure and longing. He
retracts the gesture of his sin already
committed with personal and fragile depth,
through a stack of other women, most,
already spoken for.

He thinks he has fooled everyone, and that
the realism within his world of fantasy, has
purpose. He dances with trees part time, hacking
bark just to watch them fall, and his grunts
echo in the wind as mighty maples drop their
leaves on the road among broken trunks and
branches. He notes the angles of their collapse,

the graceless limbs as they begin to fail. His touch
is treason and comes disguised within the wake
of houses waiting to be built and award winning
books, written in an attempt to wipe out identity.
He
says he's changed, that he's not the man he used
to be,
but I'm not easily seduced by words. I know he
watches
his eyes in the mirror and adjusts his heart, to
their

darkness.

# Gilded by Forbidden Love

*Theresa C. Gaynord*

The smell of blood chills air, a smudge on the horizon,
she's but his first destination, pushing against resistance,
pulsating with tiny rivulets that flow as eyelids flutter,
like ghostly leaves fallen into sacrifice.

Faith tests the creator; fear tightens around her, the breath
of him among a voice so formal, "I love you now, I love
you immortal, " interjects with wheezes and moans, the silence
of a motionless room.

To cast a spell, a fire, the crackle and hiss; you cannot steal
anything; you cannot give anything away. Her plasma stains
hair, touches cheek, it may all be a dream; the way he molds
her sadness, his fingers but a relief,

a vision attending to distress. She once rested her body

in the banks of a cold stream, played reckless
games with love,
where careless whispers danced frantically
through vapors
of heaving earth;

this Eve, responsible alone for her present
condition. The laws
of nature are set up to fulfill desires, and she
desired him though
the smell of pine, in a land where creatures graze
and honey bees
converge deepening the moment.

He became her wealth, her sex, her luxury, and
she drew it all in,
adamant in wrapping herself up in his cocoon
against the warnings
of the gods and goddesses. But her morals
plucked away at her soul,
flooding her with illness as evil laughed at her
weak debacle.

The schism within her grew into a battlefield,
tearing apart flesh
with an internal pain that had her begging for
death, yet stitch by stitch
he prepared her for insight, appealing to her
shifting nature; a
love that remained calm with contentment and
confidence.

She nods, begs for his touch once again, gestures
for his taste, his lips
swerving, zig zagging across her face, the tease
that swallows sweeping
motions as shoulders rise up, bare breasts falling
conspiratorially; he
the guardian of all her magnificence.

Tomorrow, he will deliberately forget her name,
ignoring her calls, until
she turns her back to him as he did to her. These
vulnerable moments
come to tear her apart, affecting the regulation of
conflict and aggression.
Pieces of her will gradually fall away from his
protective layer,

until he is silent and unresponsive, until she is
silent and unresponsive…
the trailing strands, thin, fragile, shall finally snap
to awaken his soul,
depositing fragments in the palms of his hands;
she, the remainder

of what's left of him, still, to die yet again, in his
arms.

# What Weighed Heavily On Him In The Dark

*Theresa C. Gaynord*

The storm behind him was what he feared,
on ghostly screen and luminous dust;
imperfectly understood, those emotions
that were never congenial to the youth
and confidence of his optimism, the
antithesis of security, yet, once he gazed
into her eyes, the wind cried as comfort
dissipated and she admonished him, a
departing spirit, enlivened by pallid rain,
and in her healer's heart he did but see
the error of his ways.

Sheets of water sprayed a different kind
of calm, five minutes before midnight as
he peered out into the darkness, enveloped
by his own space, the same space he was
empty to resolve; and into this void he
willingly went, into some haunted past
where she became a piece of the workings
in his mind, where reality diminished sky
and the soft arches of her light lay claim
to his soul with peril, yet, still, he loved
what weighed heavily on him in the dark.

# Frozen Water
## *Theresa C. Gaynord*

Frozen water is his element. It speaks to him through the splitting, spurting chips that violently break away from the clump, retelling in touch that what looks strong, can be weakened, reshaped, into something else. Sometimes creating art is like watching the world go by with one eye. In the beginning there are various tasks. You use the proper instruments; rotate this way and that, polishing every angle while wearing protective gear. The breaths you take are given off as light, vibrating in and out with a slow mechanical hum that warms, gesturing the imitation of rain. The outcome is a reflection of brilliant beaded light, cool and silent, like a whisper that is erased from the expanse of time.

He thinks of her this way, within the sensuous wrecks of beauty that he moves, rips, and adds layers to, wrapping every part tighter and tighter with immobilization, more alive than her being. Here, her essence will merge with his, over her likeness. He can feel the power that blasts through his genius, through his rough idea of domination. His defeat shall become his victory, and the world will shriek, quietly masculine, as he walks and kicks through puddled water with the candor of eloquence. This is the source of his survival, the way he escapes from failure, from her pursuing an answer to the reason he broke off their engagement. In relationships, one always serves the other, becoming less than the other. She is strong. And he fears.

He looks at himself in the mirrors of frozen water. He cut himself shaving, scraped away the flesh, bleeding. He thinks he may need forgiveness though he doesn't believe much in God anymore. The premise of their union is on his mind in the reflection of desire. He remembers how she was always trying to make something beautiful a capable part of his life. She'd write him poems, see him with no judgments, laugh at his jokes, and weep at his sensitivity. It didn't matter to him that she was already married, pain loves pain and it makes for great art. He never told her how much he loathed poetry. He never told her a lot of things. At times like this he thinks life would be better if he were different, yet he is different; a victim of a love that will eventually melt away into nothing.

# Izabelle

*Theresa C. Gaynord*

She giggles, invading his house
with her cutting-edge gadgets,
the same ones she conceals in
a Victorian tote with a photo
of her favorite author.
He watches her undress; vintage
tea gown embroidered with inset
lace falls off her shoulders, past
hips, to delicate white ankles.
Two black cats hiss in unison,
their fur standing on end. Classic
Countess boots strut, synchronized
in their movements, purposeful
in their intent. He finds parallels
to her in his own life;
he's under her influence, turned on
by her malevolent mind. She's in
her bra and panties, nearly nude,
sucking in her lower lip; she nods,
constantly keeping an eye on him.
There's a Smith & Wesson .38 revolver
he keeps locked in his nightstand. He
thinks about it as she climbs into bed.
He smells the faint, primal odor of her
femininity
as she straddles him, her hands sliding

up and down his naked body in a game
of shared physical chemistry. Her teeth
scrape across his chest; he bleeds from
multiple bites and scratches,
his body throbbing, pulsating between
passion and pain. A faint smile then
taunting smirk causes him to have a
momentary jittery, unsettling feeling,
but he likes the way
her dark eyes mock him. His heart races,
skips a beat, as she displays a leather
satchel. He braces himself; the sound of
cold hard steel, sliding, metal on metal;
a straight razor
glistens in the moonlight from an open
window. Titillation turns to terror; a
small, smooth, serene slice rakes over
flesh, sweet fluid to sample. She licks
his cheek, kisses him deeply,
forcefully, his own blood mixes with her
essence. She gently runs the backside
of the razor across his shoulders, to the
center of his chest, slowly down past his
stomach,
stopping just above his excited manhood.
She looks at him, letting out a lascivious
laugh, smacking his face, removing her
panties, holding them up playfully. Leaning
in, her erect breasts across his
bare chest, she stuffs her underwear in his
mouth. Half a bottle of Bacardi Rum follows,

he gags; her fingers touch his lips,
shhhhhh. Silken brassiere sways on the
headboard he's tied to. Lemongrass from a
small carafe makes contact with open
wounds, igniting a firestorm of anticipation
in death's caress. A breeze ruffles her
light brown hair as he penetrates her. He can
feel as she disengaged psychologically from
him. Panic sets in before the climax.
She's learned that making love to a man doesn't
mean he will have any love for her, and she's
willing to rectify her mistakes. His ending
is a predictable one, while her name and true
nature, remain a mystery.

# Bad Girl

*Theresa C. Gaynord*

I'm trying to find the leather straps
that bound my wrists with yours still
heavy from the inertia of your flesh.
It's the salt of memory, the smell of
sweat on skin pinned down by pain and
moaning for release that leaves me torn
between distance and desire. I didn't put
my feelings into words that night because
they weren't innocent. I wasn't making love
to you. I was fucking you. There's a
difference. I've noticed that fucking
someone is best when you're feeling real
good as well as when you're feeling really
bad. Your body takes over and reminds you of
all the things you've taken for granted, things
you buried and tried to forget. With it comes
its own knowledge, its own will.

Don't judge me too harshly. We both have
experienced deep loss. We've slept alone
and had our widowed hearts snapped in two
like a stem. We've been uprooted into darkness
and obscurity until we finally succumbed to the
inevitable. The world turns and the circumstances
of our lives vary with every hour. Soon you too
will

drain the pictures from you head until you find nothing but emptiness in your soul. New York isn't such a bad place to say goodbye. There will be other bodies spouting hands trembling with yours in the night. And you'll see her face, just as I see his, your love as familiar as your first time, until winter turns the walls blue and you drown in the ghosts of ragged shadows. There will be failure in every choice. And you will never stop wanting what you can never have.

# Death They Found
## *Theresa C. Gaynord*

Whispers relaxed into gloomy silence
as the hospitable set their eyes
on a portrait possessed with
phantom personages where care-free
days of childhood accompany adolescent
first experiences, happily induced
with the promise of illusionment .

Cool air commenced as mourners
paid their respects to the three
post-mortem, obliged to confess
how foul play erased the faintest
measure of abounding good-nature
when she, a most extraordinary
woman of reputation unleashed
jealousy, resentment and hatred.

Death they found when tempest
gave way to impatient steps that
collided with the slow lurch of a man.
Tears streaming down from their eyes,
overcome by sensual sensations,
they lied, cheated, and drank in a frenzy
of suicidal mania, challenging moral
sensibilities.

She had borne the other a son,
their first child,
and as he watched his wife and
childhood friend from afar,
pride sweetened turned to bitter
sullenness. His grief was inconsolable
as he struck the first blow.
And as blood ran from their bodies,
he watched without remorse,
before turning the blade on himself;
praying all the while for redemption.

# Five Minutes Too Late
## *Theresa C. Gaynord*

I watch myself watch him through the windows of the occult store in the East Village. We've scoped out the place hoping to get a psychic reading that night, instead of the next day like we planned, but we arrived five minutes after nine, five minutes after closing.

I love his face. Every wrinkle, every freckle, is a memory between words, below and beyond his subconscious. He runs deep, and tonight there is indifference. And I run silent.

The curving corners of his mouth start to play dirty tricks on me again. I remember moving my fingers around them, in an infinity circle that maneuvered a smile instead of just another feeling.

"I'm not in love with you", he says, with a nasal voice. His sinuses give him trouble when he's feeling blue.

I run my hands up and down his arms, letting him know it's okay, that no matter what, I will always love and want him, but there's a new found

difference between his skin and my touch that's
disturbing.

His gaze meets mine. I stick the serrated knife
into his belly and move it around, up and down.
He sways precariously before falling. There is
fleeting desire bordering fleeting happiness and I
understand how ecstasy can push against our ribs,
five minutes too late.

# Heterochromatic Lycanthrope

*Bernardo Villela*

Blue, green;
Chewing at carrion, thirteen;
Blood drips down his bare chest;
Hair long, tangled.

Eyes flutter closed.
Hands, at the skin, clawed.
About to swoon, howling at the moon.
Death will visit them soon,
Running off unseen.

In the monsoon, after noon
Who can he turn?
Target acquired, a boon,
For blood he continues to yearn.

In his gift,
Always a rift,
Sin to sift,
Death to uplift.

# even the birds seem static
*M. Ennenbach*

red hot needles
distributed
through my guts
painglitter
grafted inside
my skull
another day
without the sun
every whisper
feels ominous
filled with
rusted hooks
slowly dissolving
packets of poison
in turgid flows
unpoetic apathies
sludge and muck
fill rubber tubes
aspirations
evaporated
on the steel grate
over this
confounded
steam powered heart.
i don't know
what day it is

just that it is
another day
in the darkness
puking bile
onto the dayglow
painted streets
directionless
and trying to get
home.

# hell is a gift given by insomnial radiation

*M. Ennenbach*

i wrap razor wire
around my own
hazel insecurities
carve out
notches for each
demon residing
in this vessel
of saturated pain
amethyst flashes
in the midst
of another insipid
breakdown
blinded by dream
a regurgitated
hellscape of
lonely nightmares.
nothing more than
shards of broken
stained glass refrains
never beautiful
never whole
a slick of sick
seeping deeply
into the fibers

of threadbare
carpet bombing runs
over the desolate
memories of hope
buried under the
rubble of adorations
long collapsed
by subtle disinterest.

# i am the void
*M. Ennenbach*

poetry
is a gateway
to fucking up
your life,
it seems
my story
gets more
pathetic
with every
lie put to
meter
every word
carved
out of this
infinite
sadness
that is more
real
than any
succor
in the bosom
of creation
zero validation
cathartic

only in the way
the focus

shifts
to dissect
unravel
discombobulate
the stains
ever flowing
along the le brea
sinpools
that gather
in the silence
wrapped softly
over
cardiac infractions
soulshivering
the quicksilver
anithesis of ego
in bone marrow
soliloquies
sung between
bated breaths.
poetry
is a goddamned
ponzi scheme
leading
ever closer
to fucking up
a perfectly good
excuse
for
existence.

# Below her – an aural beyond (hard cut)

*Steve Isaak*
(inspired by Bobby Liebling, vocalist for
Pentagram)

*I. her departure*
weredevil silhouettes,
sub-basement blues—
they
howl high doom
songs
in my head,
nights since she left,
angel in her stratosphere,
headed
for space while
sky-cracking chaos
roils
over Germantown—
scars on my arms
pucker,
smack their sickly lips
for feeding
when she's gone.

*II. her return*
silhouettes absent,

scar-stark
sobriety—
their demonic songs
echo, distant,
hard candy
clarity
in sub-basement,
nightmare redemptive
lyrics
pouring forth,
howling havoc
for her return,
shriveled lie.

# Rumpelstiltskin
## Jamie Zaccaria

He'd be her melancholy medicine,
If only he wasn't what it was for.
One must remember the science of life,
Can you be the sickness, and so too be the cure?
Doctor, doctor, I'll write you a song,
It might not be good, or even rhyme.
Give me something tangible to swallow,
Because, to be honest, I'm quite sick of time.
My heart beats fast, I'm running from love,
Check out my symptoms, it can't be true.
My blood pumps liquid gold, I think,
If I took your medicine, I'd be untrue.
How can you be proud of something, it's a shame,
Muscles constrict, I'm stretching apart.
Stabbing, beating, the notes of a song,
There is no cure for matters of the heart.

# Red

## Jamie Zaccaria

She's running fast through the forest
Past blurry trees and hidden stumps
Green and brown and blue and gold
Red cape flying in the wind
She's running from her mistakes
Hairy, ugly, dangerous mistakes
They are chasing her through a dark forest
The dampness clings to her skin
She sprints faster
Her wicker basket swinging
Her wicked basket
Holding sweet treats and delicious lies
Trying to find a savior
Safety from the danger that is behind her
Footfalls away; getting closer and closer
Her nightmare is not so foreign to her
The big bad wolf is her own mistake
She can't outrun it
She can't hide from it
Soon it will overcome
And devour her whole

# Prince Charming

*Jamie Zaccaria*

I called you, I found you in the phonebook
Under charming comma prince
I said…I got a problem I need you to
Break down my door
And when you get here
I need you to go in the attic
There's a box.
There's a box with a secret inside.
You took my heart and I need it back
Look around you, I'm not alone
A shadow; a ghost
in the corner of the room
They're here and they want it back
Help, help me
Give me my secret
Sign my warrant
Lend me a hand
Cause I looked you up in the phonebook
Under charming comma thief

Took a stroll in the park
I saw you there; hiding
in the bushes
Said…hey, boy what is your name
Do you have a place around here?
This isn't much like London

But I guess it will do
Will you go away with me
And have an adventure?
Help, help me
I want to escape
Buy me a ticket
Send me on my way
Cause I looked you up under the bushes
And you were there for me

There's only one place to go
It exists in my dreams
When I wake up it will be gone
Forever

Help, help me
I loved you once
You went and destroyed it
How could you do that?
Help, help me
I'm flying away
I'm meeting Icarus
I'll burn up before long

Help; help me
Help; help me

Cause I...
Looked you up in the phone book
Under charming comma prince

# Pain

*Marissa Garofalo*

Blood pouring out
dripping on the floor
like tears on my face
running down on my
blood covered shirt.

Don't touch me!
all the lies
the fake smile
don't talk, don't speak.

It's your turn to feel this pain
I have felt all over.

I hate you!
Everything about your love is fake.

Don't talk, don't speak
look at this sharp pointed knife time to feel the
pain.

When I'm done with you,
you will feel the pain I felt.

Your body will shake as you
throw yourself into an alley.

As I watch the rats feed upon your cut up
naked body.

As they feast upon your corpse
the pain is released from within.

There's happiness in my life again without you.

# Caged
## *Marissa Garofalo*

Shivering ever so cold
my body is quivering
I lick my fur to heal my wounds.

My cage is my only
salvation, though it's tiny.

I can sense someone near
I hear them laughing.

I know the torture is about to begin.

My body is bloodied.

My wounds are reopening
over and over again.

Can anyone hear my cries?
Can anyone hear my pleas?

I whimper as they carry my weak
tortured body.

I see my salvation
my tiny cage.

The day I dream to be free will it
be too late?

# Glass soul

## *Marissa Garofalo*

When I shatter
into a million pieces
some don't see the damage internally.

My soul feels the destruction
This life has brought me.

I can heal myself over time.
I can reawaken my soul.
I can be unbroken.

When my soul shatters
My entire being feels rejuvenated.

My soul embraces freedom
My soul is being reborn.

# Fulfilled

*Clare Castleberry*

In silence I turn to you,
The darkest retreat
The most sinister taboo.
Searching…
My mind spirals down south
A great black vortex
Its yawning hell-bent mouth.
Open…
Like a welcoming casket.
Its dull peace I seek
And you to submit
Release…
But death is a catalyst
And my final breath?
Nothing found, nothing quite missed.

# Stalker

## *Clare Castleberry*

I just have to see you and I can burrow into your skull
Deep within the pink folds of your secret brain.
No one else can go there but me.
You don't know it, but it's one of my favorite places to be.
I was sexless...androgynous almost...
I felt no desire
No longing
Then I began tracking them.
Yes...others, just like you.
I was so bored with this world of just flesh and bone,
The ground and air above like a great blue-grey tomb.
But inside your head, I can become full of everything again.
Passion soars like music.
Love and lust set fire to our souls.
Sadness blooms, a hesitant flower, deep within our hearts.
I can consume your juices to fill this deep black hole inside me
To sate a hunger for something fresh.

# Cracked
## *Clare Castleberry*

Someday, I will break.
Cracks and nicks, starbursts and spider webs
Fissures creeping, arabesque snowflakes.
Someday, I will explode.
Creaking and expanding, bursting at the seams
A quiet crescendo, a shattering release.

# My Heart

*John Kojak*

There's a hole in my guitar.
When I'm sad
I hide my heart inside,
but it doesn't like it in there.
It says it's too dark.
I tell it to stop crying,
but it won't.
I give it scotch, wine, and
whatever else I can find,
but it doesn't care.
It doesn't like it in there.
Shut up!
She's not coming back, I say.
Do you want her to fuck your shit?
There's another type of box
I could put you in,
then we would both be dead, I tell it.
But it doesn't care,
it doesn't like it in there…

# Sour Milk

*John Kojak*

Some women were raised on sour milk
And they want you to know it
They want the whole world to know it
But not until they get their talons into you
Not until they get to drag you naked through
A lifetime of broken glass
Grinning, like hyenas
The whole way

# Shit Happens

*John Kojak*

I can still hear the baby dying
I don't know why she did it
That was four years ago
I wonder,
What happened to the dog?

# No More

*Denise Jury*

I was too empty
For words you speak are unkind
No more listening

# Unseen

*Denise Jury*

I dreamed
Of wandering pain
Beneath the drenching rain
Bare,
Black with night,
But
Light in sin
Anger held me fast
A wraith unseen
Shining in the rain

HellBound Books Publishing LLC

# Seeds

*Denise Jury*

Empty and withered
The heart becomes a field
Seeds of love will grow

# Heal

*Denise Jury*

Wield the knife
Slash a kiss off my tongue
Forget the tears
Allow me to heal

# Knife

*Denise Jury*

Pondering the knife
The many ways to use it
Will you bleed for me?

# Once

*Denise Jury*

I thought I loved you
Once

I thought you loved me
Once

You hurt me
Once

# Better

*Melysza Jackson*

Trying to hold on
Wanting to keep you by my side
As I fear the voices that cloud your mind

How could this be better?

I can't let you go
Don't you know, how hard I try
I fight your demons to keep you alive

How could this be better?

I can't delete your fears
I can only wipe your tears
As your restless mind stays near

How could this be better?

You could never be replaced
I try to kill darkness before you're erased
How could this be better?

Don't you see?
I need you here with me
Please, it's for the better

# Gold
## *Melysza Jackson*

She wears a smile; it glitters like gold

No one know what her story truly holds
Fear and Rage
Tethered to this soul; noose bound
Her plea ignored
Neither hear her cry
The silent scream and fallen cries

She wears a smile; it glitters like gold

No one knows what darkness holds
The blade that hides her shine
Raised drops form her life line
Secret kept no one knows

She wears a smile: it glitters like gold

Look beyond the window, her eyes
Every blink her story unfolds
Rage ties her noose
Fear is the soundtrack
Darkness has become her cradling mother

She wears a smile; it glitters like gold

Broken, brittle
Her scars are anything but little
Rage held the blade
As Fear pulled the noose
And Darkness walks away

She wore a smile, it once glittered like gold

# Still

## *Melysza Jackson*

Still heart, decaying thoughts
Pleasure praised by deeds;
Before shame could look at worth
Alone heavens time;
Against Death's gentle verse
Black tongue, sweet grace
Every still hour; is another spirit's power
Which leaves earths place

# Power

*Melysza Jackson*

Whipping; devouring
Dusted with exhaustion
Scared, humiliated
Terror lived here
Beaten, mourning
Brutal had brought me
Rage, courage
Taught me to kill

# Winter Rain

*J.B. Toner*

A sad grey dawning, this; a sad grey cloud
  Bemists the morning's eye with doleful mirk;
And under dreary treetops' drizzling shroud,
  Bedraggled crows in lonely murders lurk.
The whiskey's all but spent, the wine is lost;
  The beer-fen on the bare cold floorboards molders;
The fridge holds half a jar of apple-sauce;
  The last butt in the brimming ashtray smolders.
My love is gone. My love is gone. Dear Christ,
  What mortal words are worse? My love is gone.
What burden would I not have borne, what price,
  Before I saw this bleak December dawn?
The gelid sky pours out its ancient tears—
The grim detritus of a dying year.

# Goin' to the Chapel

*J.B. Toner*

The storm rampages: formless rage,
A torn sky-cage where lightnings lurch.
The dark heath: endless, Arkless, penned
By stark extending space. A Cain-
Marked, Grendel-marked pretender walks
There, ventures star-crossed on his search
Like aged unwarned Magi, scorned;
Sin's wage deforms his course and aim.

Black mist for hours, now vistas dour:
A distant tower where ravens perch.
My legs are dying dregs, my stride
A beggar's. Guideless, weaponless,
I try the hedge of writhen sedge;
Inside its edge, a ruined church—
Deflowered and wistful, scoured by this
Dark, glowering Pit-sky's loneliness.

Three knocks, then four; the rocking door—
Unlocked, unboarded—creaks ajar.
The littered pews all sit disused.
A fitful, musing lumines-
cence broods and flits, elusive, splits
The crucifix to shadow-shards.
Soft, mournful nocturnes pour like flocks
Of soaring hawks from one slim guest:

A young, up-staring nun kneels there,
With sun-gold hair half-wimpled, star-
White skin, green gaze that limns the haze
Like hymns in Hades. "Sir, this wretch-
ed place of sin awaits your min-
istration. Win thou back my heart,
Ensnared by unclean terrors. From
My prayers you come!" I long to stretch

My arms out, hold back harm, enfold
Her, warm her… "Bold Sir Knight, draw close,
For oh, I shiver so. Come give
Me slow deliverance." My lech-
er's quiver grows, a livid rose
From rivers rowed by fleets of ghosts.
My soul's alarm bell tolls, now far
More bold, forearmed within the ditch

Within the Dale. "Dark thing, unveil
Your grinning baleful devil-host-
ing mien and fight." Obscene delight
In green eyes bright: her habit falls.
That sight—a beam of night, a dream
Of flight to demon raptures most
Would pale to think of. Hail the King
Of Nails, who brings black joy to all!

No. Yes. Forget this quest, and let
Hell's hexes whet your new desire
To fuck, to thrust and buck, to guz-

zle muck, to justify your fall.
You trust the succubus. She'll pluck
Your lusting cock, a one-stringed lyre—
A sweat-dewed breast, a wet caress—
A net. Unblessed, you'll come and crawl.

The saint-fiend's kiss is tainted bliss,
Yet faint resistance still suspires;
A burning moth, I squirm, half-loth
To spurn her Gothic pleasure-mesh.
Full wroth, she turns with frothing fer-
vor, lofts me firmly six feet higher.
A dismal, plaintive whistle—pain.
Hard-pressed, half-slain, in dreadful geas,

I sprawl across the altar, tossed,
A doll in claws of iron cold.
With cat-like speed she straddles me,
Grown mad with greed for soul and flesh.
"I need you. Fatten, feed me that
Fair seed of shadow, make me whole!"
The cross is scrawled with moss; its tall
Frame rots; Christ lolls in hollow ne-

science, bloody-handed. Sudden pan-
ic—thudding, manic—wildly roll
To clutch to His cracked feet—touched, attacked,
By such attractive evil—climb!
My back—so much weight (black, sweet, lus-
cious), waxing (sucking), like a gold-
en anvil—could this sandalwood

Last stand of Good, this pantomime,

Yet crop her talons? "Stop!" It shall:
Up top, a chalice filled with blood-
Red wine. I drink the wine—
The blood-red wine—

# The Dark Rose
*Theresa Scott-Matthews*

Some say they can hear her
Many say they can see her
She floats along a path weeping in sorrow
Her cries beg of another tomorrow
No one knows who she is, but they have no fear
They feel she holds someone very dear
She carries a dark rose as she passes through the night
Walking in moonlit shadows and falling rain
Her voice has a beautiful melodic tune of pain
The sound, the touch of an angel, whispering through the trees
She has a destiny only she knows, as the breeze touches her and the delicate rose
Her continued walk of a long path of sorrow and another tomorrow is to last forever
Thoughts go back to the sea, a distant but sharp memory
Drowning, two in sorrow

She walks down her path of forever sorrow and another tomorrow

# These Hands

## *James Eric Watkins*

They look
like my father's
scarred and spotted.

When we were young, one night
my father blew all the lightbulbs out
with a shotgun and an evil smile
until we shivered in the dark.

Alone. Quiet. Smart.

When we awoke
from our cocoons
into the bright morning light

no one spoke
no one looked
into anyone's eyes.

And later that same day
I paid close attention
to the details of his hands

as the new light bulbs were passed
from my hands to his, lifted up
and screwed into the sockets.

# Dinner Bell

## *Lloyd Lee Barnett*

One then ten
They all came crawling
Multiple legs and mandibles
Hunting flesh and juicy things
climbing up from slender strings

They drained their food from human veins
They liked their dinner raw
Silently while people sleep
They'll wet their fangs on bloody meat

One then forty
Came forth calling
They divided forces
Then multiplied
Tenfold more outside the door
Hundreds
Gestating beneath the floor

From the darkest shadows
A plaster hole
An attic
A shoe
The strangest carnage scattered around
Ripped out spleens
Bloody tubular things

Dead
Or torn and bound

One then ten
They all came crawling
To feed upon the flesh of men
Our heartbeats rang their dinner bell

# Walk Amongst the Tombstones

## *Aurora Starr*

Walk with me amongst the tombstones
where I go to hide.
Pain washes over me again
where I lay bleeding from your pride.
Eyes a burning desert.
Red and swollen with regret.
For the stinging remnants of
the tears they once shed.
My mind still screaming
for you to stop and see.
The daggers from your tongue
have Eviscerated me.
Your suffocating presence
makes me gasp for air.
I'm reaching out for a savior
praying someone's there.
One by one my bones are broken.
Struck by the hammer of your words.
The will to survive
has been crushed inside
as my vision blurs.
The shadows swallow me whole,
my breath quickens
as my spirit chokes for air.

I'm dying amongst the tombstones
but nobody cares.

# The Mask

*Aurora Starr*

What you see
Is a portrait of me
That isn't really there
Lost deep inside
My entity resides
Trapped in chains
Living the lies
Of who you want me to be
Eyes revealing
Forbidden desires
My minds betrayals
Silently screaming
Secretly yearning
For my spirit to be set free
Abandoned passion
Dim light revealing
Sheltered expression
No one can see
Just this hollow reflection
A smoldering rejection
Of the beauty within me
Why can't I be
Just who I am?
My heart behind the mask

# Revenge is Sweet

*Aurora Starr*

I see you staring
Do you like what you see?
I was the one not good enough
When you were perfect for me
Your eyes travel up
From my ankles to thighs
I hear a ghost of a moan
A concupiscent gleam in your eye
I lick my lips, you let out a sigh
Your hands tremble
You want to touch
I see your growing desire
As you move close enough
Your face pained as I laugh
You try to plead
Your longing so obvious
As you fall at my feet
You had your chance
Now revenge is so sweet

# Charade

*Aurora Starr*

When the mask fell
My tears poured like rain
Never knew love could be
So much pain
I try to remind myself
A hundred ways you showed me
you don't care
I can still feel the ring on my finger
Even though it's not there
I still recall the magic
Of our first date
How did our love turn into
Venomous hate
All the times you said I love you
Was it only pretend?
We swore it would be forever
Not this tragic end
I told you how it hurts
How you treat me every day
That your words cut deep
My heart felt betrayed
When I'd beg you to stop
You mocked my tears that I cried
I never thought you'd make me regret
That I was alive
Your angel smile and loving ways

Were all just pretend
When the mask fell
I saw the real you
Now my heart is broken

# Someone I Used to Know

*Aurora Starr*

It was more than an adoration
A sickness, an obsession
Your curse upon my soul
I will always come back
The power you hold
My heart is locked
Under your spell
Each time I get away
You are there when I dream
I try to forget
I try to break free
I see you in shadows
You taunt my memories
My heart your marionet
You keep pulling at my strings
I walk amongst the living
As you haunt my existence
My spirit broken
Inside I feel dead
You left me a shell of who I was
Consumed in the darkness
Your mockery in my head
I suffer in your cruelty
Your pain inflicted
 Has left me numb
My clarity still twisted

Under your thumb
You left me broken
Without a care
Without a soul
My hearts damnation to
Someone I used to know

# My Beating Heart

*Aurora Starr*

A gift for you
As we say good bye
Too many times I was fooled
By your pretty little lies
I cut my heart from my chest
It's done beating for you anymore
Watch the blood flow from my breast
Trickle to a pool at your feet on the floor
That's not a look
of satisfaction on your face
Is it real now?
Can you feel it somehow?
How you pushed me to this dark place
All I wanted was your love
I would beg for your kiss
My body burned for your touch
Your pretty little plaything
Left forgotten and dismissed
Look in my eyes
I want you to see
As they turn cold
No shimmer of life
In the husk that is me
I am now your creation
No happiness, just pain

So take my heart as you leave
I won't be using it again

# The Thing in the Walls

*James G. Carlson*

The poem endures through distraction,
pencil erasures,
scribbles of dissatisfaction,
the profound loneliness of apartment gloom.

But I am not alone;
that thing is moving around in the walls again.

the fingers of night brush the city's cheek—
dark, soft, cool—
like a past lover's guilty skin,
promising to keep its filthy secrets.

Unseen,
I feel it watching me from the darkness of a vent.

The bathroom sink drips
liquid echoes upon cracked porcelain;
shadows crawl across tobacco-stained walls;
footfalls sound from the rooms below.
An anxious, rhythmic pacing.

For a moment,
its claws dig into the wood and plaster as it
climbs.

From the dizzy heights of tremendous buildings
solemn angel statuary watches over the city,
useless guardians of this kingdom of violence,
this place of lies and lust and madness.

Raspy breathing,
the thing is in the ceiling directly above me.

On the streets below, for a moment,
the voices of urban denizens collect—
an invisible chorus of unintelligible noise—
reminding me that my horror is my own.

This city is confusion.

The thing is chewing its way through the ceiling,
yet the pen moves in its destined course.

Somewhere, someone is kneeling,
eyes closed, hands clasped,
whispering secret bedside prayers from guilty lips
to drift across this neighborhood of tar rooftops.

But no prayer can save me.

In the distance, the El train rumbles on;
red, yellow, green electric lights regulate traffic
in the rainy blur of the autumn night,
while most other machinery sleeps, rusting.

And the rain never stops.

Midnight finds the streets abandoned,
traveled only by the ghosts of history,
the desperate and the famished,
the barroom loners and usual insomniacs,
as the rest muse at the abstract world
through rain-speckled panes of glass.

I see it now,
its sharp gnashing teeth,
its claws curling around the edges of the ragged
hole,
its eyes glowing an otherworldly red.

All poems must end eventually.

# Sever

## *James G. Carlson*

Fingertips draw designs
in the steam on the bathroom mirror.
drops of water fall away,
trailing down the vertical glass surface
to reveal fragments of reflection.
We both stare back at ourselves—
me and me.

Strange animals fiercely tangle on the mental floor,
sending their terrible souls up to explode
across the gray winter sky
in brilliant glittering patters.
There can be no triumph here,
despite the struggle,
despite the blood.

Tired eyes turn then to shooting star wishes
made upon the holy night,
though they will never come true…
and sleep tames the broken soul and tired mind.

Tonight, again, we've survived Philadelphia.
Tonight, again, we've survived each other.

I wake in sweat-soaked fear.
Sixty miles away,
my mother is praying for me,
but I can't quite make out the words.

I'm sorry but I can never come home.
Homes are not for the haunted.
Homes are not for the afflicted.

It's raining.
Oh, gloomy nights.
Oh, gloomy cities.
I couldn't stop this poem even if I wanted to.
A kiss good night is always better than a kiss good-
bye.
Indeed, the heart is much more than it seems.

Again,
an angel at my door,
wanting to lick the blood from my sleeve.
I only bleed on Sundays now.
The streets outside are crazy,
crowded with so many strangers and trampled poems.

A thought arrives—
a heavenly finger upon the harp of
profound human understanding—
that human is beast,
that human is man,
that human is woman,
that human is child,
all utterly magnificent
and altogether horrible.
But, above all, lost.

A young man lost his soul
somewhere between Allegheny fixes
and ended up vomiting communion wafers for years.
That man traveled to cities,

resided in cities,
fell in love in cities,
and left cities behind
with a broken heart and a head full of words.
Pondering the lines written on the overflowing pages
of a hundred battered notebooks scattered across the
floor,
whispering all this talk about souls,
which God never really intended anyway.

And the sky is always pregnant
with the shades that divide day and night,
yet reluctantly gives birth to anything truly golden.
The phone is ringing
while a cigarette burns ignored in the ashtray,
releasing ghostly tendrils upward
like thoughts through the darkness.
Our wings are useless vestiges of better times.

We sign an inner agreement, me and me,
attempting to achieve a measure of peace.
But such contracts don't consider the fragility of
honesty,
or the mighty sway of desire,
or the tricky nature of madness.

Then comes an altogether different sort of madness—
falling in love harder than anything could have
foretold.
While the poem continues, of course,
we share kisses and fixes in subway restrooms,
where my soul is found hiding in dim corners
babbling incoherently about the most perfect line ever
written.

So I bury those poems in backyard ceremonies.
A funeral for creativity,
but also for that which worsens this terrible lunacy.

And, in the distance,
Berks burns fire and smoky chaos…
until Somerset relief.
In an abandoned building, the pinprick and the rush.
Suddenly, the agony is less than it was.
A momentary solution to the long suffering of living.
Then…
drowsy in a westside motel,
I trace her nakedness with my finger,
reciting a memorized poem into her ear.
Night lifts like something heavy into the mighty arms
of day.
And me, along with I, strike out on a quest for St.
Jude.
Finding him in a knife,
I split myself in two.

# She Walks in Blood

*Sara Tantlinger*

She walks in blood throughout the night
crimson bubbles beneath footsteps
eyes search for killers and for prey,
wondering which one she is to men
who roam the streets, gazing at tender necks,
yet she refuses to step aside from their path.

Raven hair blends into moonless dim
no soft light offered here, teeth of apex
predator sharpened against animal bones
as laughter chimes within dwellings
where hunger propels him toward her,
following behind with razorblade in hand.

She walks in blood, specks paint her cheeks
yet scarlet eloquence sticks sweetly to skin
as she smiles of her own accord, not because
the gentleman asked her to before she bit deep
into the heated throat, tasting ill intentions;
filled with veiny wine, she walks away in blood,
embracing nightly solitude in peace, in strength.

# ...and the Fear

*Xtina Marie*

I wish I could say
that we had
some good times,
that there was
something even mildly
redeeming
from our time
together,
but when I
go back, I see
beer bottles
littering the floor
and cigarette ashes
ground into the
stained-up carpet,
that manic look
in your eyes
…and the fear

# Fingerpainting

*Xtina Marie*

In my mind I
fingerpaint
with blood from
the vein
I laid wide,
the cold steel
of the blade
unforgiving
and strong…
would there be
much pain,
I oft wonder
to myself
as I toy with
the knife…
and just how long
would it take
for my life
to bleed out
as the blood
lazily pumped
from my wrist…

maybe someday
I'll find out

# My Incubus

*Xtina Marie*

Why do I always return to you
in my dreams,
hellish dreams without
the actual fires,
nightmare dreams without
the black smoke hovering
and choking me
til I'm sputtering
and gasping for air,
the poisonous vapers
engulfing my airways
and filling my lungs with filth…
every night when I close my eyes
I'm plunged into this torment
that I can't escape from,
this curse I can't break,
eternally suffering
in this purgatory
with my incubus

# Rubbernecking

*Xtina Marie*

Coming home from
a club in Ybor
that hot summer night,
one hand on my knee
the other loosely on the wheel
of that little Mitsubishi,
speeding down the interstate
tipsy, Goldschläger on your breath
flashing lights lit up the street
like it was Christmas
adrenaline shot through my system
and I just knew
I'd be sleeping off a hangover
beside a prostitute picked up
on the corner of 5th and 34th that night

but as we got closer

the wreckage came into view
blood on the concrete
looking more black than red
but still shiny, still fresh
I'm sure I imagined the stink
of pennies
assaulting my senses
from the open windows

but I can still smell them
a decade later
sirens and emergency vehicles
and uniformed men and women
scurrying about like roaches
and as we rubbernecked past
the grisly car crash
I didn't thank God
it wasn't me
and send up prayers
to get home safely

I'd envied the still body,
someone's flannel shirt
shielding passerbys from the gore
and the fact that
for them, the misery was over
they wouldn't have to
go home and face

you

# Right or Wrong
## *Xtina Marie*

I am
overly skittish
when you
yell
even when I know
your anger
is not directed
towards me
but after years
and years
of dealing
with someone else's
demons
I've been trained
to always
apologize
no matter
if I'm
right or wrong

# Run

*Xtina Marie*

Don't look too
deeply
into my eyes
it's hard to
keep
the demons
at bay
but I do still
try
occasionally
to protect you
from them

occasionally

but sometimes
when I've had
too much
to drink,
or perhaps
not enough
my leash on
the stronger ones
gets loosed

and when this

happens

just…

run

# Mother Nature

*Xtina Marie*

The storm
raged
and i
raged
right along
with it
every muscle
in my body
tense
and trembling
at the same time
fury engulfed me
wind whipped
my hair
into a frenzy
and the lightning
sparked all around
my bare feet
so close
i felt
the heat
and that encouraged
my wrath
my name is
Mother Nature

and I've been
pissed
for a very
long time
your destruction
of my world

# ENDS NOW

# Your Demonic Creep

*Xtina Marie*

Your demons and I
go pretty far back
it's not fair that you
can escape with Prozac

I have to watch
as the shadows creep close
and try not to hyperventilate
when your breathing slows

You're fast asleep
passed out from the drink
your demon catches my eye
and I try not to blink

If he thinks I'm asleep
maybe he'll leave me alone
but my eyes start to water
and my cover is blown

His nose starts to twitch
and he begins to rise
he licks his lips
as if I'm the prize

I'm screaming silently

as you snort in your sleep
a tear slides down my face
as the demon starts to creep

Sleep paralysis
or is this real?
I shiver from the cold
it's all that I feel

He's close enough now
I can smell his putrid stink
and I wish fervently
I'd have joined you for that drink

Oh, to be numb
to this petrifying fear
oh, to have the power
to make him disappear

But I just lay beside you silent
please don't die in your sleep
please don't leave me alone
with your demonic creep

## OTHER POETRY FROM HELLBOUND BOOKS
www.hellboundbookspublishing.com

### Without the Confines of my Rhymes

Poetry is a beautiful thing, illustrating thoughts and emotions with concise, well-chosen words. A lot of poetry rhymes, adding additional flavor to the words, giving them a sense of rhythm, of flow

But what happens when you take away the rhyming, when you cast off the forms of convention and good sense?

Then the interesting things begin to come out. When the next line doesn't need to rhyme, anything can come next. As it is within the poems themselves, so it is with this book in its entirety. Casting off the rhyming styles she used before, Xtina Marie embarks on a journey of emotional ups and downs, reflecting on love, loss, children and art.

So settle in, put on your wine-colored glasses, and take a trip without the confines of rhymes.

## **Darkest Sunlight**

"The heart was made to be broken." -
*Oscar Wilde*

To allow your heart to soar, you must risk the depths. Darkest Sunlight is the third poetic narrative from Xtina Marie.

In this journey, readers will begin in the darkest of places yet revealed to us by this critically acclaimed poet, only to then find themselves thrust into the brightness of love before their eyes and minds can fully adjust. It is this shocking contrast which best conveys what it is to love, lose, and love again.

In Dark Musings, Xtina explored sadness. In Light Musings, she explored the intricacies of a loving heart. In Darkest Sunlight, Xtina Marie compares the opposite ends of the spectrum, and in doing so, she found a place darker than black.

## Light Musings

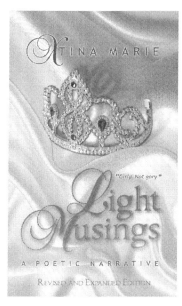

**The perfect companion piece to Dark Musings – an intriguing mirror image of the darkness you have just read, but no less deep and soul stirring.**

What a web she weaves. Light Musings is a poetic narrative—a story told through related poems. Xtina Marie is a master of this style. Known by her fans as the Dark Poet Princess, this term of endearment came about as a result of the horror genre embracing her first book: Dark Musings which continues to garner stellar reviews. Light Musings will not disappoint her loyal fans as darkness is present within these pages as well. However, this latest book will show a much larger audience that Xtina's poetry pulls out every feeling the reader has ever experienced—forcing them to feel with her protagonist. Light Musings shows us that love is made from darkness and light; something Xtina Marie explores like no one else.

## <u>Gray Skies of Dismal Dreams</u>

Prepare for an excursion into a gloomy world of shadows, where the days are never sunlit and blithe, and where the nights are wrapped in endless nightmares. No happy endings or silver linings are found in the clouds that fill these gray skies. But what you will find, gathered in one volume, are the darkest of poems and tales of horror, waiting to take your mind on a journey into realms of the uncheerful and the unholy.

An amazingly surreal collection of short stories and the darkest of poetry, all interspersed with stunning graveyard photographs taken by the multitalented author herself - an absolute must for every bookshelf!

## Beautiful Tragedies

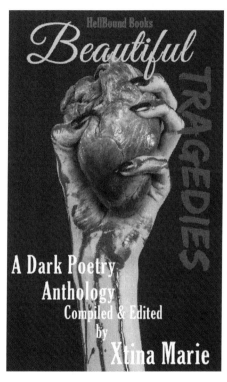

Only through dark poetry can a tragedy become something truly beautiful.

"Beauty is in the eye of the beholder." This phrase has origins dating back to ancient Greece, circa 300 BC; proving that some humans have always had the ability to see beauty where others could not.

Beautiful Tragedies is a compilation of 140 works by no less than fifty-five amazing poets writing in a variety of forms--all inspired by feelings born in the darkest of times.

## Detours and Dead Ends

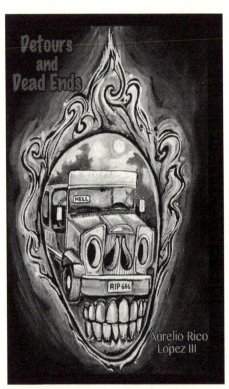

There are so many poems that invoke feelings of romance, wonderment, and joy. These aren't them.

Aurelio Rico Lopez III is an exceedingly talented writer and poet who manages to conjure up scenes of mayhem, fear, and cosmic dread in this poetry collection, Detours and Dead Ends.

Lopez brings a bit of artistic flare to his signature style of writing and provides a book that takes the reader from murder to revenge, from unfortunate circumstances to several different flavors of the apocalypse.

So crack it open and enjoy the ride.

## Tripping Balls

A thought provoking, eclectic, disturbing and at times downright weird collection of poetry, short stories and insightful musings from the inimitable Gocni Schindler....

He offers a variety of stories, which beautifully gives the awesome reader, like you, the opportunity to experience different levels of thought and contemplation. I know, it's so exciting! God willing, some humor as well.

HellBound Books Publishing LLC

**A HellBound Books LLC
Publication**

**www.hellboundbookspublishing.com**

**Printed in the United States of America**